Pokémon World

Words and Music by John Loeffler (ASCAP)/John Siegler (BMI)

Rap:

So you wanna be a master of
POKÉMON
Understand the Secrets and
HAVE SOME FUN
So you wanna be a master of Pokémon
POKÉMON
Do you have the skills to be
NUMBER ONE?

Verse I:

I wanna take the ultimate step
Find the courage to be bold
To risk it all and not forget
The lessons that I hold

I wanna go where no one's been
Far beyond the crowd
Learn the way to take command
Use the power that's in my hand

Chorus:

We all live in a Pokémon World
I want to be the greatest master of them all
We all live in a Pokémon World
Put myself to the test
Be better than all the rest

Verse II:

Every day along the way
I will be prepared
With every challenge I will gain
Knowledge to be shared

In my heart there's no doubt
Of who I want to be
Right here standing strong
The greatest Master of Pokémon

Chorus:

Rap: You've got the power right in your hands

There are more books about Pokémon.

Collect them all!

POKÉMON
THE JOHTO JOURNEYS

Secrets of the GS Ball

Adapted by Tracey West

SCHOLASTIC INC.
New York   Toronto   London   Auckland   Sydney
Mexico City   New Delhi   Hong Kong

JOHTO REGION

ISBN 0-439-22091-2

© 1995–2001 Nintendo, CREATURES, GAME FREAK.
TM & ® are trademarks of Nintendo.

Copyright © 2001 Nintendo.
All rights reserved. Published by Scholastic Inc.
SCHOLASTIC and associated logos are trademarks
and/or registered trademarks of Scholastic Inc.

12 11 10 9 8   12 13 14 15 16/0

Printed in the U.S.A.
First Scholastic printing, September 2001

1

Slowpoke, Slowpoke, Everywhere

"I need water — or I'm going to shrivel up just like these plants!" Ash Ketchum moaned.

Ash and his friends, Brock and Misty, had been walking all day in the blazing hot sun. Ash kept hoping they'd run into a lake or a stream. But everywhere he looked, he saw nothing but dusty, brown earth. There was no grass, and all the plants had withered. Clearly, this place was in the middle of a drought.

"Pika." Ash's little yellow Pokémon looked as tired and thirsty as Ash felt.

"Hey, I know!" Suddenly, Misty had a great idea. "I'll use my Staryu."

Misty fished a Poké Ball from her backpack. "Staryu, cool us off with your water gun!"

The star-shaped Water Pokémon was happy to obey. It shot an enormous jet of water into the sky. The water rained back down on Ash, Misty, and Brock, who danced around joyfully. Togepi, Misty's eggshell Pokémon, waved its arms as the cool water splashed its face.

"This feels great!" Misty exclaimed.

Before long, Ash and his friends were refreshed and ready to go. Misty returned Staryu to its Poké Ball.

"I feel way better," Ash announced. "It's time to start walking again."

Ash and his friends were traveling west through the Johto region. Ash was hoping to earn some badges by battling gym leaders. Then he could compete in the Johto League Championship. But that wasn't his real reason for visiting the West.

Ash was on an errand for the famous Pokémon expert, Professor Oak. The professor was studying a mysterious gold-and-silver Poké Ball called the GS Ball. But the professor did not know how to open the ball. He asked Ash to bring the ball to a Poké Ball maker named Kurt.

Ash had not yet made it to Azalea Town, where Kurt lived. And he had won only one badge so far. But he had recently captured a really cool new Fire Pokémon — Cyndaquil. He was sure that Cyndaquil would help him earn more Johto League badges.

Soon, Ash and his friends came to a
wooden bridge over what used to be a river.

"The river bed's all dried up," Misty
pointed out. "I bet it hasn't rained here in
months."

Brock was looking through a guidebook.
He pointed to the buildings on the other side
of the bridge. "Look, guys, there's Azalea
Town!"

Ash felt his heart begin to race. "Great!
Let's get to the gym right away!"

"Wait a second, Ash," Misty said. "We have to deliver the GS Ball," she reminded him.

"That can wait till later," Ash protested.

"The gym can wait 'till later," Misty shot back. "You promised Professor Oak you'd get that GS Ball to Kurt so we can find out what's inside. Promises are important, Ash!"

"Gym badges are important, too!" Ash shouted.

"Hey guys, there's no sense fighting about it," Brock put in. He pointed to a sign at the entrance to Azalea Town. DUE TO THE DROUGHT, ALL SCHOOLS, PUBLIC BUILDINGS, AND THE AZALEA TOWN POKÉMON GYM ARE CLOSED UNTIL FURTHER NOTICE, Brock read.

Ash's face fell. What a disappointment! Still, he wasn't about to let Misty win the argument. "Like I said," he announced loudly, "the important thing to do is to get this GS Ball to Kurt right away."

Just then, Ash noticed another sign. In fact, he noticed several. But these signs didn't have any words on them — just pictures of pink Pokémon. "What's the deal with these signs?" he asked. "They're all over the place."

"And every one is a drawing of a Slow-poke," Misty added.

"The Slowpoke aren't just on the signs," Brock pointed out. "Take a look around."

Brock was right. Slowpoke were everywhere! There were Slowpoke lying on the sidewalk, Slowpoke lounging in trees, and Slowpoke resting on the roofs of buildings. There were even Slowpoke lying across the fruit stands in front of a grocery store. Each Slowpoke had a fat, round body and a long tail with a white tip on the end.

"Wow, I've never seen so many Slow-poke!" Misty remarked.

"I wonder what they're doing here," Ash said.

Just then, Ash felt something soft beneath his foot. Uh-oh! He was stepping on a Slowpoke's tail.

Ash leaped backward. "Excuse me," he apologized. "Sorry I stepped on you, Slowpoke, but I didn't see you lying there."

Ash and his friends kept walking. A few moments later, Ash heard the Slowpoke's drawn-out wail. *"Slooowpoooke!"*

"Pika," said Pikachu, curiously.

Ash and the others turned around. The Slowpoke was groaning and holding its tail.

"It always takes a Slowpoke a while to do anything," Brock explained.

"I guess it just realized that its tail hurts," Misty said.

Out of nowhere, a boy marched up to Ash and his friends. The boy's face looked angry. "Hey, that kid hurt a Slowpoke," he announced, pointing at Ash.

"Oh, yeah," a man asked. "What did he do?"

What's going on here? Ash wondered. A

second ago, the street had been empty of people. But now, a large crowd was forming.

"Did he punch the Slowpoke?" asked another man.

"Kick it?" a woman asked.

Huh?! "I just stepped on its tail — by accident!" Ash protested.

But the angry crowd refused to believe Ash.

"He's lying!" some people shouted.

"We can't let them get away with hurting Slowpoke!" somebody said.

Ash realized that these people were seri-

ous. With a yell, the three friends turned and ran down the street.

Ash could hear the angry mob chasing after them. "What's going on here?" he asked.

"Don't try to figure it out now," Misty told him. "Just keep running!"

"*Pika!*" Pikachu agreed.

They all ran until they came to a small park. Ash was not surprised to see a statue of a Slowpoke in the center of the park.

"We lost them for now," Misty panted. "But they'll be looking for us."

"Yeah," Brock agreed. "We'd better find someplace to hide — fast!"

Robot Diglett Attack!

"*Psssst,*" someone whispered. Ash turned to see where the sound was coming from.

"Another one?" he asked. A big, pink Pokémon was emerging from behind a bush.

"Put these costumes on!" the Slowpoke said.

"Hey, that's not a real Slowpoke!" Ash realized. It was a man in a Slowpoke suit. He held out three Slowpoke suits.

"Hurry and put these costumes on," the man said. "I'll explain later."

Just then, Ash heard angry voices

nearby. The townspeople were coming! Quickly, Ash and his friends put on the Slowpoke suits. Then they sat down in front of the statue. Misty held Togepi in her lap. Pikachu posed on Ash's shoulder. The man sat next to them.

Phew, that was close, Ash thought. The angry crowd had arrived in the park.

"Hey, where did those kids go?" someone asked.

"They're not here," someone else pointed out.

"That's weird," a third person said. "Should we keep looking for them?"

"Nah, it's too hot," a kid said. "Anyway, I think we scared them away."

"Yeah, they won't show their faces around here again," another agreed.

That's for sure, Ash thought, inside the Slowpoke suit.

"Come on, let's get outta here!" someone shouted. The whole crowd headed out of the park.

Ash, Brock, and Misty pushed back the hoods of their Slowpoke costumes.

11

"Thanks, mister, These costumes saved us," Ash told the man.

"The people here in Azalea Town treat Slowpoke like gold," the man explained. "That's why they got so angry at you," he went on.

"Why are Slowpoke so important here, sir?" Brock asked.

The man peered out through the mouth of his costume and began to explain the legend of the Slowpoke. "Almost four hundred

years ago, there was a drought in Azalea Town just like this one," he said. "For many weeks, there was blazing sun and no rain. The fields dried up and the crops began to die. The people began to lose hope. Then, something amazing happened. Out of nowhere, a Slowpoke showed up in town. The Slowpoke looked up at the sky and gave a huge yawn. As soon as the Pokémon opened its mouth, the sky grew cloudy and the rain began to fall. Soon, the crops came back to life. The town was saved and the people rejoiced.

"Ever since that day," the man concluded, "the people of Azalea Town have treated all Slowpoke with great honor and respect."

"Wow!" Ash said. "Now I see why they're such a big deal here."?

"That was a pretty good story," Misty told the man. "But it doesn't explain why you're dressed up like a Slowpoke."

The man gave Misty a stern look. "There's a very good reason for that, young lady," he told her. "It's so I don't frighten the Slowpoke when I go to the . . ."

13

The man's words trailed off. His eyes popped wide open in alarm. "Oh, I almost forgot!" he exclaimed, leaping to his feet. "I don't have time for talking. I've got to get going right away!"

"Wait!" Misty shouted. "We need you to help us find somebody."

But the man was in too big a hurry to listen. He gave Ash and his friends a quick wave. "Nice to meet you. 'Bye now," he called, as he ran out of the park.

That was weird, Ash thought.

"Pika!" Pikachu agreed.

"Oh, well," Ash said. "Let's go look for Kurt."

Ash and his friends took off the Slowpoke costumes and left the park. They walked along a path until they came to a large, wooden building with a tile roof. A little girl with brown pigtails was standing in front of the building.

"Excuse me," Ash said to her. "Do you know where a man named Kurt lives?"

Silently, the girl pointed to the wooden building.

"Right here? This is perfect!" Ash exclaimed. "Now we'll find out about the GS Ball!" Excited, he rang the doorbell on the building's front door. "Anybody home?" he called.

The little girl shook her head. "He won't be back till later," she said.

"Are you his next-door neighbor or something?" Ash asked.

"No, he's my grandpa," the girl explained.

"Well, do you know where he went?" Misty asked the girl.

"He went down to the Slowpoke Well," the little girl replied. "He heard a funny noise coming from the cave, and he went down to see what it was."

Ash and the others had never heard of the Slowpoke Well. But the little girl pointed the way to a cave near the Slowpoke Park. They took off to find it.

Back near the park was a rocky hillside. Ash pointed to an opening in the hillside. He was sure he'd found the entrance to the Slowpoke Well.

Ash led his friends to the mouth of the cave. "Okay, guys, let's go find Kurt!"

"Pika!" Pikachu agreed.

Darkness surrounded them as they entered the cave. Ash and his friends crept along carefully. They hadn't gone far when they heard a loud moan.

"Pika!" Pikachu said.

"Huh?" Ash said.

"What was that?" Misty wondered

"Shhhhh!" a voice said.

"Who's there?" Ash asked. He moved toward the area the voice had come from.

Ash looked down and was startled by the sight of the man in the Slowpoke costume. He was lying on the floor of the cave, moaning in pain.

"What are you doing here?" Brock asked the man.

The man looked frantic. "I was attacked!" he told them. "A giant robot is capturing the Slowpoke!"

"Huh?!" Brock said.

"Let's go!" Ash raced farther into the cave to see what was going on. Brock and Misty were right behind him.

They stopped at the edge of a small cliff.

They could hear rumbling down below. In seconds, they saw the robot rolling toward them. It was tall and brown with a dome-shaped head. Two black eyes peered out above its big, red nose.

"Look, Ash, it's a giant Diglett!" Misty pointed out. The robot looked just like the Ground Pokémon.

"I bet I know who's inside that thing," Ash grumbled.

From inside the robot came a loud cackle. "We're inside, so prepare for trouble!" said a girl's voice. A trapdoor on top of the

robot opened and a boy and girl emerged on a platform.

"We're mean and snide, so make it double!" the boy said.

The boy and girl launched into a chant.

"To protect the world from devastation!

To unite all peoples within our nation!

To denounce the evils of truth and love!

To extend our reach to the stars above!"

"Jessie!" the girl shouted.

"James!" shouted the boy.

"Team Rocket blast off at the speed of light!" the girl screamed.

"Surrender now or prepare to fight, fight, fight!" the boy screamed.

"*Meowth,* that's right!" their Pokémon chimed in.

Ash had heard that motto a thousand times before. Team Rocket, a notorious trio of Pokémon thieves, was up to its usual tricks.

Meowth, the scratch cat Pokémon, cackled inside the Diglett Robot. Suddenly, three round panels near the bottom of the robot slid open. Three big nets shot out at lightning

speed. They headed for some Slowpoke that were sitting nearby. The roly-poly Pokémon were much too slow to escape.

"No!" Ash cried, but there was nothing he could do. Meowth used each net to scoop up a bunch of Slowpoke!

3

Nice Save, Slowpoke!

The man in the Slowpoke suit was horrified. "What are they doing with the Slowpoke?" he gasped.

"What does it look like we're doing?" James cackled. "We're stealing them!"

"Then we'll command them to make some rain for the townspeople — if the price is right!" Jessie added.

Ash couldn't believe it. "That's not fair. You can't sell people rain!" This was a really dirty trick, even for Team Rocket.

Jessie laughed. "We'll sell anything people will buy."

The Slowpoke man was panicking. "This is an outrage!" he yelled. "They have to be stopped." He tried to run toward them, but collapsed in a heap.

Brock squatted down beside him. "Hey, there, just take it easy."

But the man could not calm himself. "Save them!" he screamed.

"I'll try," Ash assured him. "Let's go, Pikachu!"

"Pika!" the little Electric Pokémon was ready for action.

Ash braced himself and started sliding down the cliff, with Pikachu right beside him.

"If you think you're gonna roll out of here with those Slowpoke, you'd better think again," Ash warned Team Rocket.

"Oh, really," Jessie sneered. "How do you think you're going to stop us?"

"Pikachu, use your Thundershock," Ash commanded.

"Not so fast, twerp," Jessie said in her meanest voice.

"Take a good look around," James chimed in. "The floor of this cave is all wet. An electric attack will shock the Slowpoke, too."

Ash hated to admit it, but Team Rocket was right. "Hold on, Pikachu," he said. "I'll have to choose another Pokémon."

"Pika." The Pokémon looked worried.

Ash grabbed a Poké Ball and threw it. "Heracross, I choose you. Stop that giant Diglett!"

Heracross emerged from its Poké Ball. *"Heracross!"* The dark-blue Bug and Fighting Pokémon stomped toward the Diglett robot.

Inside the robot, Jessie screeched. "We'll squash you like a Bug Pokémon!" she warned Heracross.

The Diglett robot began rolling forward. It rolled right into Heracross. It pushed the Pokémon backward across the floor of the cave.

Heracross raised its sturdy arms and

braced its feet against the rocky ground. It tried to stop the Diglett robot. But the robot was five times the size of Heracross. It kept right on pushing.

Ash started to get nervous. What if the robot really did squash his Pokémon?

Then, somehow, Heracross managed to get its arms under the robot. It lifted the robot high in the air and threw it hard.

Heracross was small, but it was powerful! The Diglett robot went flying end over end. Team Rocket screamed frantically.

"Meowth, do something!" Jessie ordered.

"Returning fire!" Meowth replied. A door at the bottom of the robot slid open. A flaming rocket flew out and blasted Heracross. The dark-blue Pokémon fell over in a faint.

Ash picked up a Poké Ball and called back Heracross. He knew he had to give that Pokémon a rest.

"The Diglett Mark II beat Heracross!" Meowth cheered.

"I think we've got all the Slowpoke we need," Jessie said.

"Now it's time to go make some money!" James exclaimed.

Inside the robot, Meowth pressed a button. Like the Pokémon it was named after, the Diglett robot tunneled into the ground and disappeared!

Ash's mouth fell open. He stared into the tunnel in shock. "I can't believe they're going to get away this time!"

"SLOOOOOWPOOOOKE!" Suddenly, one of the remaining Slowpoke threw back its head and howled.

Ash looked around in wonder. All over the cave, dozens of Slowpoke were emerging. They were crawling out of holes and popping out from behind rocks.

They must have been hiding from Team Rocket, Ash realized.

Slowly but surely, the Slowpoke began marching out of the cave. Ash and his friends were right behind them. Brock carried the man in the Slowpoke suit on his back.

Outside the cave, the Slowpoke climbed

to the top of a cliff and lined up along the edge. Ash and the others stood at the bottom of the cliff, watching.

"What are they doing?" Brock asked.

The Slowpoke turned their faces to the sky. One by one, they opened their mouths and yawned.

Ash remembered the story the man had told about the Slowpoke that made it rain just by yawning.

"Could it really be . . . ?" he asked.

"We'll see any second now," the man assured him.

Suddenly, the sunny blue sky turned

dark gray. "Storm clouds!" Ash exclaimed. He heard the rumble of thunder, and then the rain began to pour!

"It's true!" the man said, sounding amazed. "They really are rainmakers!"

In the streets of Azalea Town, the townspeople were rejoicing.

"Rain! Thank goodness! It feels great!" they shouted. Not one of them carried an umbrella. They were all delighted to get wet!

Only two people, and one Pokémon, were unhappy about the rain — Team Rocket!

The downpour formed a river that flowed right into the Slowpoke Well. The river filled the tunnel that the Diglett Robot was digging. The water blasted the robot through the roof of the cave. Ash watched as it sailed into the sky.

The robot crash-landed a few yards from where Ash was standing. Team Rocket crawled out, looking dazed and confused.

"I never thought we'd survive that one!" James said.

"At least we got the Slowpoke," Meowth pointed out.

"The twerp couldn't take those away!" Jessie added.

Just then, Team Rocket looked up to see Ash and Pikachu staring at them.

"I think we're in for a shock!" Jessie shrieked. Frantically, she and the others scrambled back inside the robot.

"You can run, but you can't hide this time, Team Rocket!" Ash shouted triumphantly. "Pikachu, Thundershock Attack!"

"Pikachuuuuu!" The little yellow Pokémon leaped at the robot and unleashed a powerful blast of electricity.

The Diglett robot exploded. Jessie, James, and Meowth went sailing into the sky, as they had done so many times before.

"Looks like Team Rocket's blasting off again!" they all screamed.

"We did it!" Ash exclaimed.

"Pika, pikachu!" the little Pokémon said proudly.

Ash and his friends stared up at the sky. By now, the storm had ended and a beautiful rainbow had formed over Azalea Town. On the ground, the trees and plants looked

green and healthy. A sparkling, blue river was now flowing in the riverbed.

"Do you guys really think it was the Slowpoke yawning that made it rain?" Brock asked.

"Maybe," Misty shrugged.

"Definitely!" Ash insisted.

"The world of Pokémon is filled with mysteries," the man in the Slowpoke suit said solemnly, "and this is one of the most mysterious."

"Well, the townspeople are happy now, and so are the Slowpoke," Brock pointed out.

"Yes . . . and it's all thanks to you," the man said gratefully. "You're our new heroes! Would you like a tour of the town?"

"Maybe later, sir," Misty answered. "First, we have to find a man named Kurt."

The man's eyes widened in surprise. He yanked off the head of his Slowpoke suit to reveal a head of white hair and piercing blue eyes.

Now it was Ash's turn to be surprised.

The man's face looked totally familiar, and Ash knew why. He'd seen it on the computer screen in Professor Oak's office.

"My name is Kurt," the man announced. "Why are you three looking for me?"

4

Fast Balls for Everyone

"We're here on an errand for Professor Oak," Ash explained.

By this time, Ash, his friends, and Kurt were seated around a table in Kurt's living room. Kurt's granddaughter, Maizie, was there, too. Pikachu and Togepi playfully chased each other around the room as the others talked.

"An errand for Professor Oak? Really?" Kurt asked. "Oak's the greatest Pokémon researcher in the world!"

"If he's so great, what kind of errand is this?" Maizie asked.

"You see, there's this ball that even Professor Oak can't figure out," Brock explained.

"We've been calling it the GS Ball," Misty added.

Kurt's eyes widened, and his jaw fell open. "The GS Ball?"

Ash quickly fished the ball from his pocket and handed it to Kurt. "This is it."

Kurt grabbed the ball and stared at it hard. "Why, this ball . . ." he began.

"What is it?" Misty asked.

"I have no idea!" Kurt announced at last.

Ash groaned. "You shouldn't get us all excited over nothing."

"I'm sorry, I've never seen a ball like this before," Kurt confessed. "I'll have to examine it carefully before I can say anything." He slipped the ball into his pocket and went to his workshop. Maizie was right behind him.

Ash figured he'd better contact Professor

Oak. He used Kurt's computer to make a video phone call to the professor. Professor Oak's face appeared on the screen.

"I'm here in Azalea Town with Kurt," Ash told him. "I gave him the GS Ball, but he's never seen one like it. He said he'll examine it, though."

"Well, if Kurt's got it, at least I know it's in good hands," Professor Oak said. "His skill as a craftsman is legendary. He makes Poké Balls from apricorn."

"Apricorns?" Ash had never heard of apricorns.

Professor Oak explained that apricorns grew on trees. There were some growing near Kurt's home. Apricorn Poké Balls had special features that set them apart from the Poké Balls Ash used.

Ash and his friends looked out the window. They could see several apricorn trees right there in Kurt's yard.

"That's it! I'm going to get my hands on an apricorn Poké Ball," Ash declared. Forgetting to say good-bye to Professor Oak, he ran off to find Kurt.

"Pikachu!" Ash's Electric Pokémon hurried after him. Misty picked up Togepi. She and Brock followed Ash.

They found the craftsman hard at work in his workshop. Kurt was using a long pair of tongs to place a half-finished Poké Ball into a fiery oven.

"Wow!" Ash said. Kurt's workshop was really cool. "Uh, excuse me, Kurt," he began.

Kurt turned to face Ash. "You'll have to give me some time to look at that GS Ball," he said. "I'm behind on my work."

"No, that's not it," Ash explained. "It's just that . . . I want an apricorn Poké Ball!"

"Ash!" Misty scolded. "Watch your manners. You can't just ask for something like that."

"Now, now, that's okay," Kurt assured her. He grabbed three Poké Balls and handed them to Ash and his friends. "Here you go. Consider these thanks for helping me out at the Slowpoke Well."

"Thank you, Kurt," Ash said. He examined the Poké Ball in his hand. The bottom, white half looked like a regular Poké Ball.

But a white dot and a yellow lightning bolt decorated the red half of the ball.

"So, this an apricorn Poké Ball?" Ash asked.

"Those are all Fast Balls, made from white apricorns," Maizie piped up.

"Fast Balls?" Ash asked.

"Yeah," Maizie explained. "It's best for using on Pokémon that can run away quickly.

"Apricorns come in seven colors," she went on. "There are white, red, blue, black, pink, green, and yellow. So the Poké Balls made from each kind have different-colored markings on them. And they each do something different."

Ash's eyes lit up. "Really? I want to get Poké Balls made from other apricorn colors, too!"

Misty scowled. "You shouldn't be so greedy, Ash."

"If you really want some, I'll make some for you," Kurt put in. "All you have to do is bring me the apricorns."

"We only have white apricorns in our garden," Maizie said, "but you can find other colors in the hills behind our house. I'll take you there."

"Great!" Ash was really excited. "Come on, Pikachu. Let's head for the hills and get some apricorns!"

5

Brock Catches a Pineco

"This is a green apricorn," Maizie explained. "You use these to make Friend Balls."

The apricorn looked like a round, green fruit that was the size of a Poké Ball. A dark cap sat on top of the apricorn and attached it to the tree branch.

Maizie turned to Ash. "You can take some of these apricorns."

Finally! Ash thought.

Maizie had led Ash and his friends to the hills. Now, she was pointing out the various kinds of apricorn trees.

41

Ash was eager to gather apricorn in all seven colors. But so far, his mission wasn't working out too well.

The first tree they had seen was a pink apricorn tree. But the apricorn weren't ripe, so Maizie had forbidden Ash to pick them.

Next, they had come to a yellow apricorn tree. Ash really wanted some yellow apricorn because they were made into Moon Balls. According to Maizie, Moon Balls were good for catching Pokémon that evolved using Moon Stones. It was just what Ash needed to catch a Clefairy.

Ash was all set to pick a yellow apricorn when Maizie spotted some Pokémon on the tree branches. Ash stared at the small, prickly, gray Pokémon. He took out Dexter, his Pokédex.

"Pineco, a Grass Pokémon," said the pocket computer. "It appears calm as it hangs sedately from tree branches, but it will Self Destruct at the slightest provocation. Pineco are very difficult to raise."

"Difficult to raise? I'm up for that challenge," Brock said. He moved to the tree so he could capture one.

Instead, Brock tripped. All the Pineco

exploded, charring the tree. Then they dropped to the grass, still sizzling. That was the end of Ash's quest for yellow apricorns.

I'm gonna get some green ones for sure, Ash thought. "Let's go Pikachu!" He stepped toward the green apricorn tree.

"Pika, pika!" The little Pokémon cried out in alarm.

"Beedrill!" Ash shouted. Out of nowhere, a large swarm of the flying, black-and-yellow striped Pokémon had appeared. Each

Beedrill had two sharp stingers on their front legs, and one yellow stinger on its tail.

"Run for it!" Brock screamed. The group raced out of the apricorn grove, with the angry Beedrill right behind them. Ash and the others had to leap off a small cliff to escape the swarm.

"That was close," Ash panted. "I didn't know gathering apricorns would be this hard."

"Making Poké Balls is more work than you might think," Maizie replied proudly.

Maizie pointed to another tree filled with blue apricorns. "Blue apricorns are used to make Lure Balls," she explained. "You can use those to catch Water Pokémon."

Maizie let Ash and Misty pick one blue apricorn each. Ash was excited to get his first apricorn. But he wanted more.

Next Maizie led them into another grove of black apricorn trees.

Black apricorns are used for Heavy Balls," Maizie explained. "Heavy Balls are good for catching really heavy Pokémon."

"Oh, yeah? I'll take one of those, too," Ash said, jogging toward the tree.

"Huh?" Ash stopped running when he noticed several Pineco hanging from the tree branches.

"Now's my chance to get one!" Brock exclaimed.

Ash knew Brock was proud of his ability to handle the toughest Pokémon. If Pineco were difficult to raise, Brock would prove he could raise one.

"Which one will it be?" Brock wondered, staring up at the Pineco. He counted off the Pineco one by one. "Eenie, meanie, miney, moe. Catch a Pineco — oh, no!" A heavy gust of wind was blowing the Pokémon out of the tree. Frantically, Brock grabbed one and hugged it tightly in his arms.

"Team Rocket!" Ash had spotted the source of the sudden windstorm. Jessie, James, and Meowth were back, with another crazy contraption.

"Behold, our Economy Edition Apricorn Harvesting Machine!" James said.

Ash and his friends stared at them scornfully. This machine was just an ordinary old fan, powered by a bicycle built for three.

"Prepare for trouble," said Jessie.

"Make it double," said James.

"We'll blow all the apricorns clean out of the tree!" Jessie shrieked.

"I can't wait to collect them all!" James added.

"This is going to be a breeze!" Meowth joked.

Team Rocket pedaled furiously. The fan blew harder and harder. More Pineco flew out of the tree. Soon the apricorn would be flying out, too.

"You won't get away with this. Pikachu, get them!" Ash shouted.

Pikachu let loose a Thunderbolt. But the electricity only increased the fan's power.

"We are ready for you this time," Meowth cackled.

"Oh, no!" Ash groaned.

"Pineco!" Brock yelled. The Pineco that Brock was holding wriggled free from his arms. It bounced over to Team Rocket and flung itself at them with all its might. *Oof!* All three of the apricorn thieves were knocked off their bike.

"Look what you did," Jessie screeched at the Pineco. She grabbed a Poké Ball and threw it hard. "Go, Arbok!"

Jessie's purple cobra Pokémon exploded from the ball and lunged at Pineco. The smaller Pokémon leaped out of Arbok's reach. It hopped away frantically, with Arbok in hot pursuit.

"I think that Pineco's going to self-destruct," Ash warned. The Pokémon looked just like those others did before when Brock startled them and made them explode.

"Stop it, Pineco," Brock called to it.

"The Fast Ball!" Maizie exclaimed. "Use

48

the Fast Ball Kurt gave you to catch that Pineco."

Quickly, Brock threw the Poké Ball. The Fast Ball opened wide and captured the Pineco just as Arbok lunged at it. Startled, the purple Pokémon crashed into the ground headfirst.

"That's as far as you're going to get, Team Rocket!" Ash shouted.

"Go, Arbok!" Jessie screeched.

The big purple Pokémon leaped at Ash and his friends.

"Pikachu! Use Quick Attack and Tackle!" Ash ordered.

"Piiika!" Pikachu raced at Arbok, sending the giant Pokémon scurrying back to Team Rocket.

"Pikachu, Thunder!" Next, Pikachu blasted Team Rocket and their Pokémon with a tremendous bolt of electricity. This time, the blast was so strong it blew up the Apricorn Harvesting Machine and sent Team Rocket sailing into the sky.

"Looks like Team Rocket is blasting off again!" they screamed.

"We did it!" Ash shouted.

"Pika!" Pikachu agreed.

Maizie thanked Ash and the others for his help.

But Brock didn't need any thanks. Ash could see that he was thrilled with his new Pineco. Ash still wanted one more apricorn.

"Ouch!" Something small and hard hit Ash on the head and plopped into has hand. Ash couldn't believe it. It was a black apricorn!

"Maybe that's the tree's way of thanking

51

you for saving the apricorn from Team Rocket," Misty guessed.

Maizie led the group back to Kurt's workshop.

Ash examined his new apricorns. He wondered what new Pokémon he might be able to catch with his apricorn Poké Balls.

Back at the workshop, Kurt took the apricorns from Ash and Misty. "I'll make these into fine Poké Balls," he said.

"Thank you, Kurt," Ash said.

"By the way," Brock asked, "did you discover anything new about the GS Ball?"

Unfortunately, Kurt had not. "I don't know who made it or where," he explained, "but it's protected by a strange lock. I've never seen such a system."

Ash wondered what Professor Oak would say. But Kurt had a plan.

"No one knows more about Poké Balls than I do. I will get to the bottom of this," he promised. "If you don't mind, please leave the ball with me a little longer."

"Sure, I don't mind," Ash replied.

"Just let Professor Oak know if you find anything new," Brock suggested.

Misty looked relieved. "Finally, our part in this mission is over."

"Now it's time to get some badges," Ash added happily.

"Pika!" Pikachu agreed.

"That reminds me," Kurt said. "Now that the drought is over, the Azalea Gym is open again!'

"Really? All right!" Ash exclaimed. "Let's go, Pikachu!"

6

Cyndaquil vs. Spinarak

"How do you think you will do in your Pokémon match?" Misty asked Ash.

Ash, Brock, and Misty were walking along the road into Azalea Town. Misty was pretending to be a reporter. She was holding her water bottle like a microphone, and using it to interview Ash.

Ash held his head high. "I predict victory," he answered Misty. "How about you, Pikachu?"

"Pika, pika," Pikachu agreed, from its perch on Ash's shoulder.

"I don't know, Ash," Misty said. "I think this will be a tough one."

"Why?" Ash asked.

"Just think," Misty explained. "In your other gym matches you could always count on Charizard to use its firepower to win when you made dumb mistakes."

It was true. Ash hadn't been in a gym battle since he'd left his Charizard behind. It was now at a Charizard Preserve, where it would get special training. But Ash was not worried.

"No problem. Charizard may be gone, but my Cyndaquil's got plenty of firepower," Ash said.

Moments later, Ash and the others arrived at the Azalea Town Gym. At least, they thought it was the gym. The building was made of glass panels, like a greenhouse.

"Hello," Ash called, as they wandered inside. He looked around. Tall, leafy trees and lush, green plants were everywhere.

"Brock, are you positive we're in the right place?" Misty asked. "It looks more like a garden than a Pokémon gym."

"Well, according to the guidebook, this is the Azalea Town Gym," Brock assured them.

"Let's have a look around," Ash suggested. "The gym leader's got to be around here someplace."

Misty looked really nervous. "It feels to me like something creepy's going to jump out at us any second now!"

Ash thought that was silly. "What kind of something?"

Misty shuddered. "Probably some kind of slimy, slippery — aaahh!"

A little green Caterpie with big black eyes and red feelers jumped right out at Misty.

Misty shrieked. "Oh, I don't like Bug Pokémon, I don't like them at all," she wailed, covering her head with her arms.

Ash didn't see what all the fuss was about. How could anyone be afraid of a cute little Caterpie?

"This isn't a Pokémon gym," Misty complained. "This is a torture chamber!"

"Wrong," said a voice from somewhere in the treetops.

Ash and the others looked up, startled. A

boy was sitting on a tree branch high above them. He had dark, bobbed hair and wore a green shirt and shorts.

"You have come to the right place. This is the Azalea Town Gym, " he informed them. "And how rude of you to say you don't like Bug Pokémon. Don't you know that Bug Pokémon are the best Pokémon of all?"

"Just who do you think you are, anyway?" Misty asked.

"You should be the ones telling me who you are," the boy shot back.

"I'm Ash Ketchum, from Pallet Town," Ash expained. "I came here to have a match with the Azalea Town Gym Leader."

"So you're another challenger," said the boy. "I'm Bugsy, the leader of the Azalea Town Gym. Bug Pokémon are my specialty."

Ash was ready to go. "Let's battle!"

Bugsy led them through the trees to an open area. White battle lines were laid out on a dirt field. A man with short brown hair stood on the sidelines. Ash knew from his uniform that he was a judge.

The judge stepped out into the middle of

the field. "The official battle between the Azalea Gym leader, Bugsy, and Ash, from Pallet Town, will now begin," he boomed. "If Ash wins, he will earn a Hive Badge."

The judge explained the rules. "Each trainer may use three Pokémon. If a Pokémon faints, it is out of the competition. Are both players prepared?"

"I'm always prepared," Ash replied. *I've been ready for this battle for weeks,* he thought.

"I'm ready too, Ash," Bugsy said. "Have

you heard the phrase, 'He who controls Bug Pokémon controls the world'?"

Ash most certainly had not. He scowled. "Who said that?

"I did." Bugsy hurled a Poké Ball. "My first choice will be the silent soldier of Bug Pokémon. Go, Spinarak!"

Ash eyed Bugsy's Pokémon. It was green, with spindly, black-and-yellow striped legs, and two red horns sticking out of its face. "A Spinarak, huh? Then, Cyndaquil, I choose you!"

Ash threw a Poké Ball. Out came a small, blue-and-tan Pokémon with a long nose and red spots on its back. Cyndaquil was little, but it could shoot out huge flames once it had warmed up. Ash hoped Cyndaquil was up for the battle today. A Fire Pokémon was his best bet against a Bug Pokémon.

"All right, Cyndaquil, turn on your engine!"

"Cynda!" The little Pokémon looked eager to please.

"Spinarak, String Shot!" Bugsy commanded his Pokémon.

The green Pokémon shot out a stream of sticky white thread. It didn't look very scary. But Ash knew Spinarak could use the thread to make a cocoon around Cyndaquil so it wouldn't be able to move.

"Dodge it, Cyndaquil!" Just in time, the quick little Pokémon leaped nimbly out of the path of the String Shot.

"Continue String Shot!" Bugsy shouted. Spinarak kept shooting sticky string. But Cyndaquil dodged every attack.

"Spinarak! Cover the entire area with String Shot!" Bugsy shouted.

Spinarak flew at Cyndaquil. It shot a
long, looping stream of thread that landed
on and around the Fire Pokémon. When
Cyndaquil tried to move, it stepped on the
thread and got its feet stuck to the ground!

"Oh, no!" Ash groaned. "Cyndaquil, use
Flamethrower!"

Cyndaquil tried, but Ash could see that it
just wasn't ready. It produced only a few
harmless puffs of smoke from the red spots
on its back.

"Spinarak! Poison Sting!" Bugsy ordered.

The green Pokémon flew at Cyndaquil and blasted it with a series of toxic liquid darts.

Poor Cyndaquil was still stuck firmly to the ground. The Fire Pokémon was powerless to dodge Spinarak's attack.

Bugsy grinned triumphantly. "Spinarak, finish it off!"

The green Pokémon sailed toward Cyndaquil again. Ash knew there was only one thing to do. He was going to need Cyndaquil later, when the Pokémon was ready to use Flamethrower. But that meant he had to rescue it now, before it fainted. He grabbed a Poké Ball.

"Return, Cyndaquil!"

chikorita Gets Tough

"That showed good judgment," Bugsy told Ash.

Ash knew Bugsy was right. He had done the right thing by giving Cyndaquil a rest. But now Ash had to choose a new Pokémon. Most of his team was weak against Bug Pokémon.

He grabbed a Poké Ball. "I'm going to have to win this on guts alone," Ash said. "Chikorita, I choose you!"

"Chika!" Chikorita leaped into Ash's arms and cuddled him. The little Pokémon was

pale green with a darker green leaf growing from the top of its smooth head. It had a ring of green dots around its neck.

Bugsy was shocked by Ash's choice. "A Grass Type against a Bug Type?" he questioned. "What kind of stinky decision is that?"

Even Brock and Misty looked skeptical.

Ash looked at Chikorita. "Forget about type," he assured the little Pokémon. "I battle by instinct, and I have faith in you."

"Chika!" the little Pokémon agreed.

"I have pretty good instincts, too, and mine tell me Chikorita's going to lose," Bugsy declared. "Spinarak, String Shot!"

"Dodge it, Chikorita!" Ash countered.

The little Grass Pokémon was quick on its feet. It zigzagged back and forth, evading every one of Spinarak's sticky strings.

It was time to go on the offensive. "Now, Chikorita! Vine Whip!"

Two long vines shot out from the ring of green dots on Chikorita's neck. The little green Pokémon tried to use the vines on Spinarak, but it was Spinarak's turn to

dodge. The Bug Pokémon used a stream of sticky thread to latch onto a tree branch and swing away from Chikorita's vines.

"Excellent, Spinarak," Bugsy praised. "Now use Poison Sting!"

"Don't give in, Chikorita. Razor Leaf!" Ash ordered.

Chikorita nodded its head. Three razor-edged leaves went spinning through the air and stopped Spinarak's poison darts.

Keep going, Ash told himself. *Think fast.* "Chikorita! Stop Spinarak with Sweet Smell."

Chikorita's leaf stood straight up on its head. Spinarak flew at the Grass Pokémon, straight into a sweet-smelling cloud. The Bug Pokémon's eyes glazed over. Spinarak collapsed into a heap. Chikorita's attack had the sweet smell of success!

"No!" Bugsy groaned.

Yes, Ash thought. "Now, Chikorita! Tackle!"

Chikorita charged at the helpless Spinarak and rammed it hard. Spinarak fell over in a faint.

"Spinarak!" Bugsy shouted, running to its side.

"Spinarak is unable to battle," the Judge declared. "Chikorita wins."

Next, Bugsy chose his Metapod. The green cocoon Pokémon had a crescent-shaped body. Ash knew that Metapod was the evolved form of Caterpie. Someday, it would evolve into Butterfree. But in its present form it couldn't do much more than Harden and protect itself from attacks. Ash wondered what Bugsy's strategy was.

"I can't believe you beat my Spinarak," Bugsy said. "But just watch my Metapod, the pride of all Bug Pokémon warriors!"

Ash wasn't worried. He turned to Chikorita. "We'll take this battle, too! Go, Chikorita, Vine Whip!"

Chikorita raced at Metapod with its vines extended.

"Metapod, Harden!" Bugsy screamed.

Metapod flashed bright white, then turned green again. But now its green coating looked shiny and hard.

Chikorita's vines whipped against Metapod, but had no effect. Metapod just sat there calmly.

"Don't give in, Chikorita," Ash encouraged. "Razor Leaf!"

"Metapod, Harden," Bugsy commanded once more.

Chikorita's sharp leaves were powerless against Metapod's steely hard body. The leaves hit Metapod squarely, but bounced right off.

Ash grimaced. If Metapod kept using Harden, he'd never weaken it. He had to keep trying. "Go, Chikorita, Razor Leaf again!"

"Metapod, Jump!" Bugsy quickly countered.

Even Ash had to admit that Metapod's jump was awesome. The Pokémon sailed high into the air, over Chikorita's head.

"Metapod! Tackle!" Bugsy commanded.

Tackle? Ash had never seen a Metapod use Tackle before. This wasn't good.

"Chikorita!" Ash screamed.

Metapod roared down from the sky and landed, hard, on top of Chikorita.

"Chiiiikaaa!" the little Pokémon wailed. It flew through the air, into Ash's waiting arms, and fainted.

"Chikorita is unable to continue battle," proclaimed the Judge. "Metapod wins."

Ash thought about his next move. Chikorita was out. Cyndaquil was still in rotation, but it was weak. He had to beat Metapod and one more Pokémon if he was going to win that Hive Badge.

He did not come all the way to the Johto Region to lose.

Ash knew one Pokémon that never let him down. "Pikachu, help me out!"

"Pika!" Lightning danced from Pikachu's rosy cheeks. As always, the little yellow Pokémon was ready for action.

The judge called for the next round to begin.

"Metapod, Jump, then Tackle," Bugsy immediately demanded.

"You won't get away with that twice," Ash replied. "Dodge, Pikachu!"

Pikachu leaped nimbly out of Metapod's

path. The green Pokémon hit the ground so hard that it sent up a giant cloud of dust. The dust was so thick that Ash and Pikachu couldn't see a thing.

"Tackle!" Ash heard Bugsy yell. Suddenly, Metapod came flying through the dust, headed straight for Pikachu. In the nick of time, Pikachu dodged it.

Metapod was moving too fast to stop itself. It flew toward a tree, and disappeared into thin air!

"What was that?" Ash yelled.

"It's all speed," Bugsy explained, as Metapod reappeared and came flying around the tree. "Nothing can match a Bug Pokémon that's gained speed."

"Oh, yeah? If it's speed you want, Pikachu's even faster," Ash bragged. "Pikachu, Agility!"

"Pika!" Pikachu stuck its front legs out and soared at Metapod. The two Pokémon flew around and around each other in circles. Finally, Pikachu grabbed Metapod in its front paws.

"Now, Pikachu!" Ash shouted. "Thunder-bolt!"

"Pika!" Pikachu hung on tightly to Meta-pod and unleashed a mighty bolt of light-ning. Metapod's whole body glowed. Finally, Pikachu let go. Metapod collapsed onto the ground.

Bugsy ran to his Pokémon's side. "Meta-pod?"

The Judge could see that Metapod had had enough. "Pikachu wins," he declared.

"Good old Pikachu," Misty said.

"Yeah, those two really do work well to-gether," Brock added.

Ash grinned at his trusty Pokémon. "Good work, Pikachu."

Now Bugsy was down to his last Poké-mon. "You're good, Ash," he admitted. "It's been a long time since a trainer has gotten this far against my Bug Pokémon."

The gym leader pulled out a Poké Ball. "But you don't stand a chance against my number three. It's an elegant Pokémon war-rior," he bragged. "Go, Scyther!"

Brock and Misty gasped. "It looks like the real battle starts here," Misty said.

Scyther was a fearsome, green Pokémon. It stood five feet tall on two big feet, with a head like a dragon's and two huge wings. Scariest of all were Scyther's arms. Each one had a long, shiny silver blade at the end.

Ash felt a little scared. But he wasn't about to show it. "We'll hit first and win fast. Pikachu, Agility!"

"Pika!" Boldly, little Pikachu raced toward Scyther. The big, green Pokémon barely reacted. It just stood there and stared, as if it couldn't believe that such a tiny creature was challenging it.

"Pika?" Pikachu stopped short. It looked up timidly at Scyther.

Ash could tell the little Pokémon was losing its nerve.

"Come, on, Pikachu, Thunderbolt!"

Those words were all it took for Pikachu to rally. *"Pika!"* The Electric Pokémon flew though the air toward Scyther.

Bugsy responded quickly. "Scyther, Double Team!"

Ash couldn't believe his eyes. First one extra Scyther, and then two, appeared in front of Pikachu. "Don't be fooled, Pikachu! Hit each one with an Electric Attack."

"Pika-chu-chu-chuuuu!" One by one, Pikachu blasted each Scyther. The two extra Scyther disappeared.

But the original Scyther was still standing. "Scyther, Slash!" Bugsy yelled.

Pikachu tried desperately to escape as Scyther flew toward it. But Bugsy's Pokémon went after it with a vengeance. Over and over, Scyther swiped at Pikachu with its long, sharp claws.

"Pikaaaa!" With a desperate cry, Pikachu fell to the ground and fainted.

"This round goes to Scyther," said the judge.

Ash ran to Pikachu and scooped it up in his arms. "Pikachu, are you okay?"

"Pika." The little Pokémon was going to be fine. But right now, it needed to rest. Ash

had only one Pokémon left. He grabbed for a Poké Ball, hoping his choice would not let him down. "Come on, Cyndaquil. Light your flame right away."

"Cynda," the Pokémon chirped. Cyndaquil was even smaller than Pikachu. And right now, it looked very mild. Despite Ash's command, it wasn't producing any fire at all. Not even a wisp of smoke.

"I don't even need a strategy against an opponent that won't attack," Bugsy sneered. "Scyther, end this match with Slash!"

"Scyther!" The giant Pokémon roared as it tore after Cyndaquil with bladelike arms flying.

"Dodge, Cyndaquil!"

If Cyndaquil had one strength — besides fire — it was speed. Again and again, Scyther lashed out at Cyndaquil with its vicious razor arms. One solid hit would take Cyndaquil out of the match for good. But Cyndaquil was too quick for that. Again and again, it dodged each swipe.

"Good job, Cyndaquil," Ash encouraged. "Keep dodging, just like that."

79

Ash only hoped that Cyndaquil wouldn't grow tired. If it slowed down, it would have no chance against Scyther. Then, all at once, four little patches of fire shot out from the spots on Cyndaquil's back.

"Its flame has finally lit!" Ash shouted triumphantly.

"Scyther, Double Team." Once again, there were two extra Scyther. All three of them went after Cyndaquil, slashing away with their six razor-sharp arms.

But Ash was no longer worried about his Pokémon. "Once Cyndaquil's flame is lit, Bug Pokémon are nothing. Cyndaquil, Flamethrower!"

"*Cyyyynndaaaa!*" Cyndaquil let out a mighty yell as it torched the Scyther with a river of fire that streamed from its mouth.

Two of the Scyther vanished into thin air. "All right!" Ash shouted. "The one left is the real one!" One more good blast, and that one would be gone, too.

"Scyther! Swords Dance!"

Scyther spun in circles the air, holding

its sword-like arms in front of its face. A wind whipped up around Scyther as it spun.

Cyndaquil's flame blasted the swords. *Excellent,* Ash thought. Then something strange happened. The fire bounced off of the spinning wind and blew right back at Cyndaquil.

"*Cynda,*" the little blue Pokémon moaned. It tumbled through the air and landed flat on its back in the dirt.

8

Bye, Bye, Bugsy

"Cyndaquil, are you okay?" Ash ran to his Pokémon's side.

"Cynda!" The little Pokémon jumped to its feet. The flames on its back crackled and grew higher.

Ash breathed a sigh of relief. "You can still go on, then?"

"Cynda!" Ash could tell that Cyndaquil was ready for action. But what strategy should he use? "If we use Flamethrower, it'll just get blown back at us again."

"Fire Attacks are a Bug Pokémon's greatest weakness," Bugsy said with a smirk. "Don't you think I knew that and was prepared? Scyther is trained to repel fire perfectly."

"I see now," Brock said. "When Scyther builds its strength for Swords Dance, it spins like a fan. The wind it creates repels the attack."

Ash frowned. "There's got to be a way to bring Scyther down . . ." he mumbled.

Suddenly, inspiration struck. "That's it!" Ash shouted.

"Scyther! End it with Fury Cutter!" Bugsy ordered.

"Cyndaquil, get your Flamethrower ready," Ash countered.

Bugsy sneered. "I told you that wouldn't work. Scyther, Swords Dance!" The powerful green Pokémon began to spin.

"All right, Cyndaquil," Ash commanded. "Jump right above Scyther."

Cyndaquil made an awesome vertical leap. It dangled in the air above Scyther.

"Now point your body straight down!" Ash went on.

Cyndaquil turned upside down, with its snout pointing toward the ground.

"What?" Bugsy looked totally confused.

"Now, Cyndaquil! Flamethrower!" Ash shouted.

"Cyyyyndaaaa!" An enormous flame engulfed Scyther from above.

Ash's plan had worked perfectly. The winds were spinning *around* Scyther, not *on top* of it. By attacking from overhead, Cyndaquil had a clear shot.

"Scyther!" Bugsy screamed.

"Quick, Cyndaquil! Use your Tackle Attack."

Cyndaquil charged through the air. It smashed into Scyther as hard as it could. The Bug Pokémon was still stunned from the Flamethrower Attack. It collapsed to the ground in a faint.

"Scyther is unable to battle. Cyndaquil wins the round," the Judge declared. "Victory goes to the challenger from Pallet Town!"

"We did it, Cyndaquil!" Ash shouted.

"Pikachu!" the Electric Pokémon chimed in.

Cyndaquil danced around proudly. *"Cynda, cynda!"*

Bugsy walked up to Ash. "Ash," he said. "I was quite confident in Scyther's fire defenses. I never imagined someone would attack the way you did. You competed well."

Bugsy held out his hand. "Here," he went on. "This Hive Badge is yours."

Ash examined the badge. It was round and red, with three black spots. It looked sort of like a Ledyba, a cute Bug Pokémon. Ash grinned. "All right! I earned a Hive Badge!"

Ash and his friends said good-bye to Bugsy. They were on their way out of Azalea Town when Ash suddenly remembered something. "What about those apricorn we left with Kurt? He said he'd turn them into Poké Balls for us."

As if she had read his mind, Kurt's granddaugther, Maizie, appeared in the road. She waved to Ash and his friends. "Don't forget these!" she called.

Ash and the others went to greet her.

Maizie held three strange-looking Poké Balls in her hands.

Two of the balls were half white and half blue.

The third ball was white on the bottom and black on the top. Four blue circles decorated the black half.

"The two blue ones are Lure Balls," she explained. "The other is a Heavy Ball."

Ash and Misty took the Lure Balls, and Brock took the Heavy Ball. They all thanked Maizie and asked her to thank Kurt for them, too.

Maizie smiled. "Stop by the house anytime you're around," she told them. "We may just know something about that GS Ball by then!"

"We will," Brock promised.

Maizie said good-bye and headed back to Kurt's.

"Let's get going for real this time," Ash said.

"Where to next?" Misty asked.

Ash put the Lure Ball in his backpack, along with the Fast Ball Kurt had given him earlier. He tucked the Hive Badge inside his vest.

He couldn't believe everything that had happened during the last few days. He had earned his second Johto League badge. He had two amazing new Poké Balls that he was itching to try out. His Johto journey was turning out to be full of surprises.

"Let's just head down the road and see where it leads us," Ash answered Misty. "I'm sure wherever we go, something exciting will happen!"

POKÉMON

GOTTA READ 'EM ALL!

POKéMON

GOTTA READ 'EM ALL!™